P9-CAP-882

Disney's Adventureland

Including *Robin Hood and the Daring Mouse,*
The Sword in the Stone: The Wizards' Duel, The Aristocats

A GOLDEN BOOK • NEW YORK
Western Publishing Company, Inc., Racine, Wisconsin 53404

© 1989 The Walt Disney Company. Stories and illustrations in this book previously copyrighted © 1974, 1970, 1963 The Walt Disney Company. All rights reserved. Printed in the U.S.A. No part of this book may be reproduced or copied in any form without written permission from the copyright owner. GOLDEN, GOLDEN & DESIGN, A GOLDEN BOOK, and A GOLDEN TREASURY are trademarks of Western Publishing Company, Inc. Library of Congress Catalog Card Number: 89-84576 ISBN: 0-307-15752-0/ISBN: 0-307-65752-3 (lib. bdg.)

B C D E F G H I J K L M

Robin Hood and the Daring Mouse

Friar Tuck frowned as he came into his little church. "Alackaday!" said he. "Prince John has raised the taxes again."

Oliver Mouse, the friar's tiny helper, stopped dusting the keys of the organ. It was hard to be so small, but Oliver felt important when Friar Tuck told him his problems. "We'll have good times again when King Richard comes home," Oliver said hopefully.

"Indeed we will, or my name's not Robin Hood!"
said a brisk voice from the back of the church.
Friar Tuck and Oliver both smiled at the sight of
Robin.

"When King Richard comes home, I won't be an outlaw anymore," said Robin Hood. "I'll be able to marry Maid Marian, and we'll live happily ever after."

Robin's friend Little John came ambling into the church. "That'll be nice, old buddy," he said, "but right now we *are* outlaws. We take from the rich and give to the poor, remember?"

Little John held up a bag that jingled. "Here's a bit of money for the needy folk of Nottingham," he told Friar Tuck. "Want to see that it gets to them?"
The friar chuckled. "I'd love to!" he said.

Robin Hood and Little John left the money with
Friar Tuck and hurried off to Sherwood Forest.
   "Can I help give away the money?" Oliver asked.
   "It would be nice," said Friar Tuck, "but you're
very small, Oliver. You couldn't carry much."

It was true. Oliver *was* small—so small that people hardly ever noticed him.

Oliver noticed people, however. When he looked out of the church door, he noticed the sheriff of Nottingham striding up the street. "Friar Tuck," he cried, "the sheriff's coming this way!"

"Good heavens!" said Friar Tuck. "He must be trying to collect more taxes!"

"Hide the money!" shouted Oliver. He was so excited that he ran around in circles. "Hurry! I know— hide it in the poor box!"

"Good idea!" declared Friar Tuck. "Even the sheriff wouldn't be wicked enough to break open a poor box."

But Friar Tuck was wrong, for the sheriff stamped into the church and went straight to the poor box. He began to pry at the lock with his dagger.

"You can't do that!" shouted Friar Tuck.

"Oh, but I can," said the sheriff, and he wrenched the lock off the box.

"Aha!" he said when he saw the golden coins that were heaped up inside the box.

"You can't take that money!" said Friar Tuck. "It is for the poor!"

"Then I'll give it to poor Prince John," announced the sheriff.

"Prince John isn't poor!" squeaked Oliver.

Friar Tuck was so angry that he snatched up his staff and took a mighty swing at the sheriff.

"Traitor!" cried the sheriff as he ducked.

His guards ran into the church. They pulled Friar Tuck's hood over his head. They broke his staff. Then they clapped chains on him and led him away.

Poor Oliver was frightened. He wanted to creep into the hole in the wall, which was his home. He wanted to hide behind the organ.

However, brave Oliver scooted out of the church and followed the sheriff and his men. They didn't notice.

Brave little Oliver followed the sheriff across the drawbridge and into the great, grim castle of Nottingham.

He kept close to the wall. He saw Friar Tuck thrown into the prison.

Oliver crept to the prison door. "Friar Tuck? Friar Tuck, it's me. It's Oliver." Oliver peered in through the iron bars, and he gasped. No wonder, for he saw that every poor villager of Nottingham was locked in the prison.

"What happened?" asked Oliver. "Why are all of you in prison?"

"We couldn't pay our taxes," said poor Widow Rabbit.

"Run away, Oliver!" warned Allan-a-Dale, the minstrel. "Hide, before they catch you."

Oliver did run. He ran as far as the drawbridge. But then he saw the sheriff, and for once the sheriff *did* notice him.

"Don't hurry off," said the sheriff. "You haven't paid your taxes, either." With that, he dropped Oliver into an empty barrel in the courtyard.

Oliver looked around and saw high above him a little hole in the side of the barrel.

"If only I could reach..." he thought. Oliver jumped as high as he could. Again he tried, and again, until finally he was able to grasp the side of the hole.

"Perhaps it's a good thing to be a very small mouse," thought Oliver. Then he pushed and squeezed and struggled and, at last, forced his way out.

"I'll get Robin Hood!" Oliver said. "He will know what to do."

He scampered past the guards on the drawbridge. They didn't notice him. Oliver ran straight to Sherwood Forest, as fast as he could go.

Oliver knew that Robin Hood would be in the
secret place beyond the waterfall. It had seemed only a
whistle away when he rode there in Friar Tuck's pocket.
But now that he was running on his own short legs, it
was a long journey. He ran on and on, until, at last, he
saw Robin's campfire.

"What news, Oliver?" asked Robin Hood, who *always* noticed Oliver.

Panting, Oliver told Robin about the wicked sheriff and about the villagers locked up in the prison.

"We'll see about that!" said Robin Hood.

"You bet we will!" added Little John.

That night, Robin and Little John climbed the walls
of Nottingham castle. And who was with them? Oliver,
of course. He was riding in Robin's hat.

Oliver's little heart sank when he saw that the sheriff
was sitting right outside the prison door. But Robin
noticed that the sheriff was asleep. So Oliver carefully
took the sheriff's big iron key, and Little John, without
even waking him, unlocked the prison door.

Quickly, Robin Hood, Little John, and Oliver freed
the villagers. Everyone ran off to Sherwood Forest to
hide and wait for good King Richard to come back to
England.

When he did come home at last, the villagers
flocked back to Nottingham, where Robin and Maid
Marian were married in Friar Tuck's little church.

Of course, Oliver played the wedding march on the
organ—and, of course, *everyone* noticed. For one thing,
he played very nicely. For another, he was a brave and
daring mouse, and one *does* notice a brave and daring
mouse.

The Sword in the Stone
The Wizards' Duel

Once there was a boy named Arthur, but everybody called him Wart.

One day he saw some birds flash by the window.

The birds frisked about gaily in the sunshine. Poor Wart had to stay inside the dark tower and study his lessons. He gave a deep sigh.

"Wart," said Merlin, who was his teacher, "whatever you learn, learn as well as you can. Get back to your lessons, boy."

Wart said, "I wish I were a bird."

Now, Merlin was a wizard and good at changing people into different things. "I think I'll grant your wish," he said. Merlin stood up and, pointing his wand at the boy, chanted a magic spell.

At once Wart began to shrink. He grew smaller and smaller and smaller.

And suddenly he changed into a little sparrow!
His arms were feathered wings. His body was tiny
and covered with gray and brown feathers. And he had
a squeaky, birdlike voice with which to sing and chirp.

"I'm a bird!" chirped Wart.
His tiny body shook with joy.
"I'm a bird! Watch me fly!"
With that, he launched himself
from the tower window. And with
widespread wings he glided
smoothly through the air.

Wart taught himself many more flying tricks. Soon he was a swift and graceful flyer.

He was flying along, admiring the clouds, when a black speck showed in the sky. It was a hungry hawk.

"Wart!" cried Merlin from below. "Watch out!"

With a flick of his wings, Wart darted away.
The hawk followed him, its huge dark wings beating
strongly. It was a long, long chase.

But the feeble little sparrow escaped by dropping
down a chimney.

Exhausted, he fell to the bottom of a cold and sooty fireplace. "Where am I?" he wondered.

Just then, he saw a funny old witch peering at him.

"Well, look who's come to visit Madam Mim," she said, cackling, "a little sparrow!"

"Oh, please. I'm really a boy," chirped Wart. "Merlin changed me with his wonderful magic."

At this, the old witch shrieked with laughter.

"Merlin's magic is dreary and dim—when compared to the magic of Madam Mim!" she said.

Just then, the witch heard her name called.

"Who's that?" she cried.

In a puff of smoke stood Merlin.

"Madam Mim," he said, terribly stern, "let
Wart go."

The witch gave a gurgling laugh. "Try to make me,
dear," she said. "I challenge you to a wizards' duel, to
take place immediately!"

Nodding grimly, Merlin accepted the witch's challenge. Soon they were outside and ready to duel.

Wart sat down on a tree limb and gave a puzzled chirp. "What's a wizards' duel?" he wondered.

Merlin answered him. "Madam Mim and I will change ourselves into different things in order to destroy each other."

When Wart heard this, he began to shiver.

Meanwhile, Madam Mim and Merlin had drawn their wands.

"Ready," howled the witch.

"Get set..."

"*Duel!*"

Madam Mim started the duel by changing into a crocodile.

In a flash Merlin became a tiny turtle and hid inside his hat.

And when the crocodile found
him there, Merlin changed into a
rabbit and nimbly hopped away.
Changing into a fox, the witch
chased the rabbit.

But then Merlin changed...

into a hunting dog,

and *he* chased the fox!

Madam Mim changed from fox to tiger, only to find
that the dog had changed into a sharp-clawed crab.
Furious at having her nose pinched, she turned
into...

a sharp-horned rhino!

　　As a mouse, however, Merlin easily slipped by the lumbering rhino.

But then, calling on her blackest magic, Madam
Mim changed into a fearsome, flame-spewing dragon.

Wart gulped with dismay.
Whatever could poor Merlin change into now?

Merlin changed into a tiny germ.

The tiny germ carried a rare illness called purple pox, which was very catching.

In a flash, the dragon broke out all over in a rash of great purple spots.

Anyone sick with purple pox had to stay in bed for two whole weeks.

And so Merlin clearly was the winner of the wizards' duel.

Quickly, Merlin changed himself and Wart back into people.

"Sir," Wart asked him after they had put Madam Mim to bed, "how did you ever learn such powerful wizardry?"

"When I was a boy," answered Merlin, "whatever I learned, I learned as well as I could."

"Oh," said Wart in a small voice.

Merlin chucked him under the chin. "Wart," he said fondly, "get back to your lessons."

"I will, sir," said Wart. "I will!"

The Aristocats

In Madame Bonfamille's fine home in Paris, all was peaceful. Well, almost....

"Me first!" Kitten Marie shouted. "I'm a lady!"

"Ha! You're not a lady," said her brother Toulouse.

"You're just a sister," said Berlioz.

"I'll show you!" Marie shouted.

Marie chased after her brothers. The chase brought giggles and then tears, as Marie's tail somehow ended up in Berlioz's mouth.

"Children!" said Duchess, their mother.

"I was just practicing my biting, Mama," said Berlioz.

"Aristocats do not bite," said Duchess. "Come, let's practice being ladies and gentlemen."

Soon all was peaceful again—but not for long. Out in the kitchen, someone was planning to do something bad to the Aristocats.

Edgar, the butler, had heard Madame say many times that she was leaving her fortune to her dear cats and that Edgar could have what was left after they were gone.

Edgar had thought, "Four cats. Nine lives each. Four times nine is... is... too long. They'll outlive me, unless..."

And, right then and there, Edgar planned a way to make the Aristocats disappear.

"Come, kitties," he called. "Come taste this delicious *crème de la Edgar*."

It *was* delicious. Their friend Roquefort the mouse thought so, too. But...everyone who drank it fell asleep!

And the Aristocats slept *so* soundly that they didn't know they left home in a basket on Edgar's motorcycle.

They didn't know that Edgar was chased by dogs, and that the basket fell off and landed under a bridge.

They didn't know they were alone, far out in the country, until a storm broke, and they woke up.

"Mama!" Marie called out. "I'm afraid! Where are we?"

"I don't know, darling. I...I...let's just try to sleep until morning."

But Duchess couldn't sleep. All she could do was worry.

Then she heard a rough voice singing, "I'm O'Malley the Alley Cat. Helpin' ladies is my—"

"Oh, Mr. O'Malley, can you help me?" Duchess asked. "I'm in great trouble. I'm lost."

O'Malley bowed. "Yer ladyship, I'll fly you off on my magic carpet for two."

Berlioz popped up. So did Toulouse. And Marie. "What magic carpet?" they asked.

"Uh…er…" O'Malley stammered. Then he grinned. "Look, I said magic carpet for two, but it can be a magic carpet for *five* also." He made an **X** on the road. "It'll stop for passengers right here. Watch!"

They watched. Something came down the road. O'Malley made himself big and scary-looking and jumped out in front of it. The something stopped right on the **X**.

"All aboard!" said O'Malley. "One magic carpet, ready to go."

"Aw, it's just a truck," said Berlioz.

"Shh!" said Duchess. Then she smiled at O'Malley. "It's a lovely magic carpet. Is it going to Paris?" she asked.

"It's goin' somewhere," said O'Malley, helping her on.

But soon the driver of the magic carpet saw that he had passengers. He stopped with a jerk. He threw things. His passengers jumped to safety.

"What an awful man!" said Duchess.

"Humans are like that," said O'Malley.

"Oh, no, Mr. O'Malley," said Duchess. "My humans aren't like that."

"Hmm!" said O'Malley. "Then how did you get here? Somebody doesn't like you."

Duchess thought about that as they began the long walk back to Paris.

Finally, they arrived in the city, so tired they could hardly take a step.

"We'll stop and rest at my peaceful pad," O'Malley said.

But the peaceful pad was bouncing with sound. "Oh...uh...friends have stopped by," O'Malley explained. "We'll go somewhere—"

"I'd like to meet your friends, Mr. O'Malley," said Duchess.

So O'Malley introduced all his swinging musician
friends. What fun it was! They played for the four
Aristocats, and Duchess sang for them.

Then, after the children were tucked in, Duchess and O'Malley talked.

"Your friends are delightful," said Duchess.

"How about sharin' them?" asked Mr. O'Malley. "I mean, how about stayin' here with me? Like forever."

Marie heard him. She whispered, "Mr. O'Malley's going to be our father... maybe."

"Great!" said Toulouse.

"Shhh!" said Marie. "Listen!"

"Oh, if I only could!" said Duchess. "But I can never leave Madame."

"She's lucky," said O'Malley. "I never felt that way about a human, and no human ever felt that way about me." He sighed. "But... well, I'll take you home."

The next day, O'Malley watched as Edgar opened
the door for the Aristocats.

"Oh!" said Edgar. "You're back! I mean... uh, how
nice to see you back!"

"Looks like they don't need me anymore," said
O'Malley. He turned away sadly.

But O'Malley was wrong. The first thing Edgar did
was put Duchess and her children into a bag. Then he
heard Madame call, "Are my little dears back? Did I
hear them?" Edgar popped the bag of cats into the
nearest container and went to answer Madame's call.

The four Aristocats were stiff with fear. What would happen to them now? Then Duchess remembered Roquefort the mouse. "Get O'Malley!" she called. She told him how to find her friend. "Hurry!"

Roquefort ran out, just as Edgar came back in with a trunk.

"Now," Edgar said, "you're going in this trunk to Timbuktu and *never* coming back! Onto the baggage truck you go and away forever." He opened the door.

But suddenly alley cats were everywhere. They unlocked the trunk and let out the Aristocats.

Then they put Edgar inside. Now someone else was on his way to Timbuktu!

SEND TO
TIMBUK

And there were some happy cats who were very glad to stay home. Listen! You can hear a rough voice, and a lovely soft voice, and three little voices singing... "We're Mr. and Mrs. O'Malley. We're the *five* Aristocats."